D0445524

DRAGONBREATH

REVENGE OF THE HORNED BUNNIES

DRAGONBREATH

REVENGE OF THE HORNED BUNNIES

BY URSULA VERNON

DIAL BOOKS

an imprint of Penguin Group (USA) Inc.

*This one's for my dad, who explained to me what a jackalope was,
and then that they weren't real, and then why anybody would make one
in the first place, and then what "gullibility" and "profit motive" meant,
back when I was younger than Danny.*

DIAL BOOKS
An imprint of Penguin Group (USA) Inc.
Published by The Penguin Group • Penguin Group (USA) Inc., 375 Hudson Street, New York,
NY 10014, U.S.A. • Penguin Group (Canada), 90 Eglinton Avenue East, Suite 700, Toronto,
Ontario, Canada M4P 2Y3 (a division of Pearson Penguin Canada Inc.) • Penguin Books Ltd,
80 Strand, London WC2R 0RL, England • Penguin Ireland, 25 St. Stephen's Green, Dublin
2, Ireland (a division of Penguin Books Ltd) • Penguin Group (Australia), 250 Camberwell
Road, Camberwell, Victoria 3124, Australia (a division of Pearson Australia Group Pty Ltd)
Penguin Books India Pvt Ltd, 11 Community Centre, Panchsheel Park, New Delhi - 110 017,
India • Penguin Group (NZ), 67 Apollo Drive, Rosedale, Auckland 0632, New Zealand (a
division of Pearson New Zealand Ltd) • Penguin Books (South Africa) (Pty) Ltd, 24 Sturdee
Avenue, Rosebank, Johannesburg 2196, South Africa • Penguin Books Ltd, Registered Offices:
80 Strand, London WC2R 0RL, England

Designed by Jennifer Kelly
Text set in Stempel Schneidler
Printed in the U.S.A.

10 9 8 7 6 5 4 3 2 1

Library of Congress Cataloging-in-Publication Data
Vernon, Ursula.
  Revenge of the horned bunnies / by Ursula Vernon.
      p. cm. — (Dragonbreath ; 6)
  Summary: Danny Dragonbreath is excited about going to camp with his best friend Wendell
and classmate Christiana even though his obnoxious, seven-year-old cousin Spencer is going
too, but things change when Spencer finds a real jackalope.
  ISBN 978-0-8037-3677-1 (paper-over-board)
  [1. Camps—Fiction. 2. Cousins—Fiction. 3. Animals, Mythical—Fiction.
4. Dragons—Fiction. 5. Iguanas—Fiction. 6. Humorous stories.] I. Title.
PZ7.V5985Re 2012
  [Fic]—dc23   2011015605

SHERIFF DRAGONBREATH ENTERED THE CANYON WITH HIS SIX-GUN IN HIS HAND.

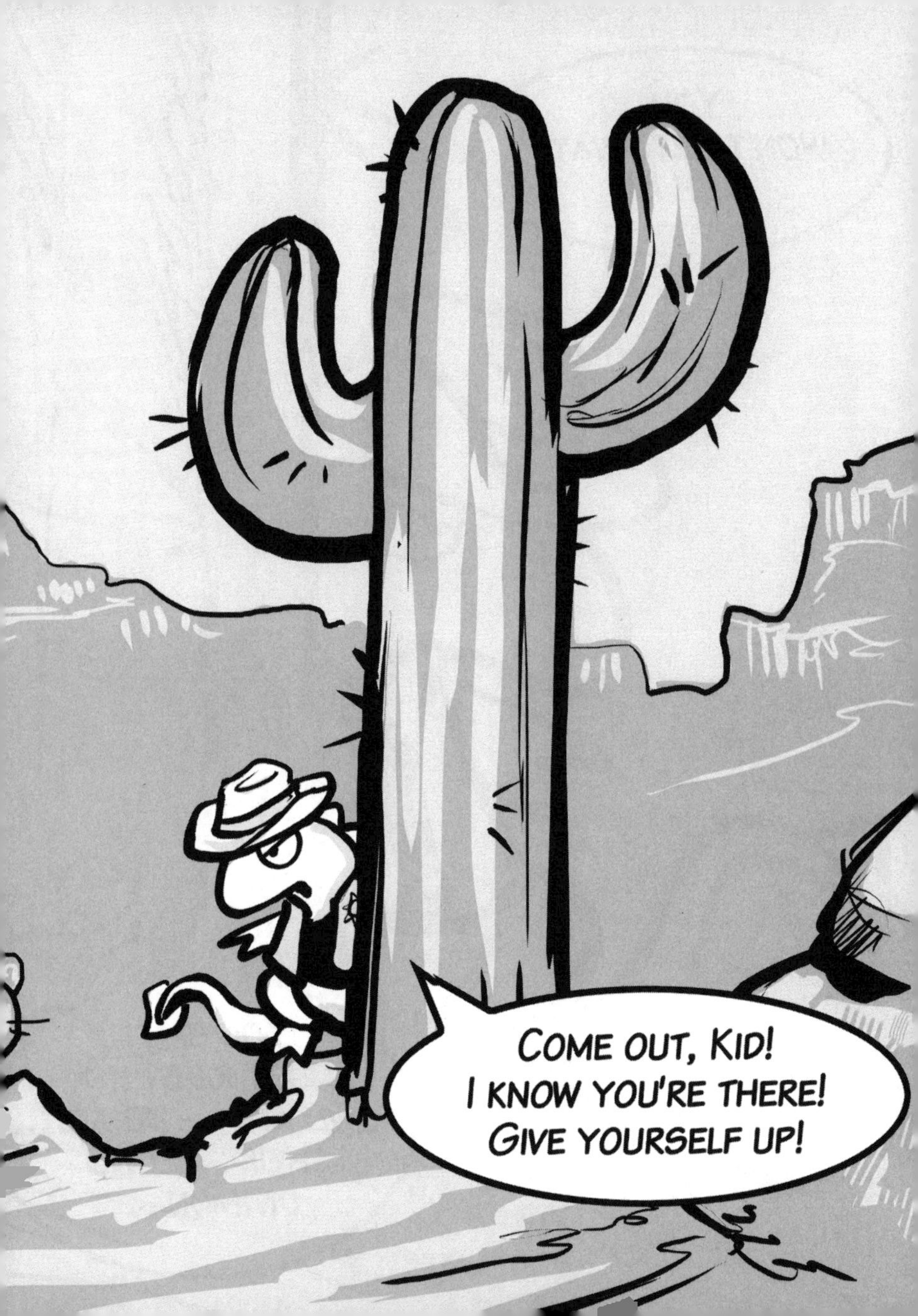
COME OUT, KID! I KNOW YOU'RE THERE! GIVE YOURSELF UP!

OF CAMP AND COUSINS

Danny Dragonbreath had a great imagination, much to the dismay of his parents, his teachers, the lunch lady, and the occasional ambulance crew.

Even he, however, had a hard time imagining his best friend, Wendell the iguana, as a desperate outlaw. Wendell would never ride into a town and shoot it up, and given the choice between holding up a train and determining how fast a train leaving Cincinnati going sixty miles an hour would take to catch up to a train leaving an hour earlier and going forty-five miles an hour . . . well, Wendell would take the story problem every time.

Danny put his snout in his hand and thought about this. If Wendell wasn't the outlaw . . . no, he couldn't be the Indian either. The last time Wendell's mother had caught them playing cowboys and Indians, she'd read them a twenty-minute lecture on the history of Native American oppression, which had really put a damper on things. It was hard to have a thrilling shoot-out while yelling: "I respect your position and hope that we can come to a mutually respectful conclusion!"

Wendell's mother did *not* understand about things like this.

Danny reluctantly gave up on being Sheriff Dragonbreath. It didn't matter anyway. He was going to summer camp in three days, and

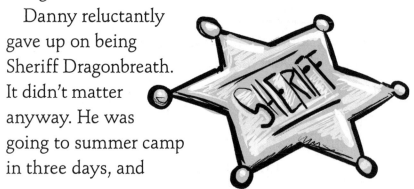

absolutely nothing could ruin his mood. There would be swimming and hiking, and he'd get to ride a horse like a real cowboy. Plus, there would be sagebrush and cactus and campfires and roasted marshmallows for *a whole week.*

Wendell had gotten permission to go, which was awesome, and apparently Christiana Vanderpool, the know-it-all crested lizard, was also going, which was probably okay. Christiana still didn't believe that Danny was a dragon, but she had to believe in cowboys. There was definite proof that cowboys existed.

Camp was going to be so cool. Maybe they'd even find gold in the desert! Outlaws buried their gold sometimes, didn't they?

OR WAS THAT PIRATES . . . ?

Either way, nothing could spoil his excitement. He loved summer camp.

And then at that moment, his mother came into the room and spoiled his excitement.

"Spencer?" asked Danny weakly.

"Yes. Your aunt Shirley just called and told me the news! Spencer's crazy about you, you know."

"Mom, *no!*"

Danny did not like his little cousin Spencer. He supposed he probably wouldn't want Spencer to be eaten by ravenous eels, but that was only because his aunt Shirley was pretty nice and sent good Christmas presents (never socks and underwear), and having her son eaten by eels would make her sad. On the other hand, if Spencer were merely *kidnapped* by ravenous eels and forced to work in an eel-owned salt mine, that would be just fine with Danny.

Spencer was one of those annoying people who would sit on the couch while Danny played video games and keep up a running commentary about what Danny should do next, what he was doing wrong, how many lives he had left, and how his friend had played this game way better and gotten through this bit way faster. He would intersperse this commentary with random statements like "Lava is made of fire and rocks!" and "If you were as light as a feather, somebody could kill you with one punch, probably." His statements had no bearing on anything and didn't even make *sense,* and whenever Danny died in the video game, Spencer would make a *wa-waaaaah* noise.

He couldn't even tell Spencer to shut up, because his cousin was a tattletale and would run to Danny's mom and aunt Shirley to say that Danny was being mean. So Danny had to grit his teeth instead of breaking the controller over Spencer's head. Then when Spencer finally left, Danny's mom would poke her head in the doorway and say, "It's so *nice* that you and Spencer get along so well."

It is a cruel injustice of childhood that if you are related and born within five years of each other, your family assumes that you should be friends and play nicely together, regardless of how you and the other kid in question might feel.

"Mom," said Danny. "I am going to be absolutely reasonable here."

"Mom. You cannot send Spencer to camp with me. He will ruin everything. I realize that you think we're buddies, but Spencer is *horrible*."

"First off, I'm not sending him, his mother is. And second, I realize he might be a little annoying at times, but he's really excited that you'll both be going to camp together. The least you could do is make an effort."

Danny groaned. There it was: "Make an effort." That was his parents' answer to most of the woes afflicting him. Can't breathe fire? Make an effort. Failing math? Make an effort. Beets for dinner? Make an effort.

The world's most obnoxious seven-year-old about to destroy the single best week of summer? Make an effort.

"Mooooommmm!" said Danny, which hardly ever worked, but was worth a shot.

"You'll live," said his mother mercilessly. "Frankly, you should just be grateful *you* get to go to camp, after the Bottle Rocket Incident last year."

Danny felt this was unjust. Camp Jackalope was in the desert! Who knew so much of it would be flammable?

And anyway, this was clearly only a tactic to distract him from the issue at hand:

Danny tried to look wounded. His mother snorted and tossed a pillow at his head.

"You'll be fine," she said. "Look, you don't have to stay with him every waking minute, but I do want you to keep an eye on him. This is his first time at camp, and he might be homesick."

"My life is *ruined,*" said Danny, determined not to let her change his mind. "I might as well *die.*"

"Truly, my heart bleeds for you." His mother

stepped out of the room. "If you decide to stay among the living, though, we're having mac and cheese tonight. With hot dogs in it."

Danny grumbled. His summer vacation was ruined. It would be a wonder if he didn't expire of sheer disappointment.

After dinner, of course.

The next few days passed so quickly that Danny barely had time to worry about his cousin. There were clothes to pack and sleeping bags to find and towels to wash. And then his mother went through his duffel bag, and not only did she confiscate all of his fireworks and most of his comic books, she insisted on packing the bag full of far less vital stuff, like socks and underwear.

Despite the lack of explosives and the addition of Spencer, Danny couldn't help being excited on the morning of departure. The buses left from the parking lot of the community college, and there was already a large turnout of campers, parents, and harried-looking people trying to stuff suitcases into the buses. Danny spotted Wendell through the crowd, talking to Christiana, and waved them over.

"Hey."

"Hi."

"Yo."

"Any sign of your cousin?" asked Wendell in an undertone.

"Nothing yet."

"Maybe aliens got him," said Danny hopefully. "In a UFO."

"Unlikely." Christiana looked down her snout at him.

"Most UFOs turn out to be weather balloons or the planet Venus."

"I don't mind if the aliens take him to Venus. I bet Venus is very nice this time of year."

"Don't look now," said Christiana, "but there's a short kid who looks like you coming this way."
Danny sighed.

Spencer looked at Wendell, looked at Christiana, dismissed both of them as uninteresting, and turned back to Danny. "Did you ever beat *Poison Sands*? 'Cos my friend Alan did."

"Yes," said Danny. "I did. Ages ago." (This was not, strictly speaking, true. Danny had gotten to the very last boss and been beaten twenty-three times in succession, whereupon he had finally looked up the hints and found out that he was missing a crucial item and would have to replay the last three hours of the game. This was so frustrating that he had decided to go play outside and by the time he thought about the game again, he'd lost the disk under a pile of dirty laundry.)

Wendell, who knew all about this (except for maybe the bit with the laundry), said, "Yeah, he tore through it. I saw him." Wendell was a *very* good friend.

"So, Christiana," said Danny, attempting desperately to change the subject, "this is your first time at Camp Jackalope, huh?"

"Yeah," she said. "The waiting list for space

camp this year is so long that Dad said I'd just have to pick something else."
She shrugged.

IT'S WAY COOLER THAN SPACE CAMP! I BET THEY DON'T TOAST MARSHMALLOWS OR RIDE HORSES AT SPACE CAMP!

Wendell shoved his glasses farther up his snout. "There are crafts," he told Christiana, in much the same tone that a doctor in a movie would say "There is smallpox in the village."

"I suppose that was inevitable." She considered.

"Still, it probably won't be all bad. There are nature walks and stuff. Nature is good."

DID I MENTION THAT YOU GET TO RIDE HORSES? LIKE REAL HORSES?

"They don't have any video games," said Spencer. "I read the brochure. You're not even allowed to bring them."

"Well, no," said Danny. As much as he loved video games, he hadn't really missed them at camp before. You were generally too busy trying to start a fire with tinder and flint or trying not to fall off a horse to think about it.

"I wish my mom wasn't making me go," said Spencer glumly. "I told her I didn't want to."

This put a rather different face on things, but before Danny had a chance to absorb it, the suitcases were loaded and whistles were blowing and it was time to get on the bus.

ATTACK OF THE CHEERFUL COUNSELORS

It was a three-hour bus ride to Camp Jackalope. Danny spent most of it staring out the window and trying not to listen to Spencer.

"So in this TV show, then, the alien, right— well, he's the kid, but he's got an alien in him, and, and, the bad guy has a death ray and it's wired to go off as soon as the alien hatches—"

Death rays, thought Danny bleakly, had never been so boring.

He envied Wendell and Christiana. Spencer had scooted into the seat next to Danny before anyone could protest, and so Wendell

and Christiana were sitting together, swapping comic books. Christiana did read comic books, although she tended to get very sarcastic every time Super Skink swooped and caught someone who was falling from a great height. "They'd impact just as hard on his arms as they would on the pavement," Danny could hear her saying irritably. "It's not like momentum goes away just because you're a superhero. Super Skink's costume would have a lot of splattered tourists on it."

Danny ordinarily would have argued that Christiana was missing the point. But compared to Spencer's nonstop monologue about every TV show he got to watch, the notion of Super Skink cleaning tourists off his spandex was positively fascinating.

SO THEN IT TURNS OUT THAT THE WOMAN WHO HIRED THEM WAS ACTUALLY THE ZEBRA SMUGGLER ALL ALONG!

Danny tried reading a comic book. It did not go well. Spencer had a friend who'd read it, and the friend said it wasn't very good and if you wanted

to read a *real* comic book you should totally read the *Fishslinger* series and had Danny read the *Fishslinger* series because Spencer had and what was his favorite character because Spencer liked Odamagong the ninja manatee and did Danny like ninjas?

Danny was not crazy about ninjas, because of the incident with the ninja frogs some time ago, but he didn't feel like getting into this with his cousin, who would either call him a liar or tell his mother.

Danny also wished his parents would get more than basic cable, because some of the shows sounded pretty cool, especially *Squids vs. Aliens Across the 12th Dimension,* even if Spencer had done his best to ruin the plot retelling it.

And then, wonderfully, magically, FINALLY the bus pulled around a curve, and there was Camp Jackalope!

"We're here!" said Danny, interrupting Spencer's latest recitation. "Guys, we're here!"

"What's a jackalope, anyway?" asked Spencer, peering at the sign.

"A rabbit with antelope horns," said Danny.

"Cool! Will we get to see one?"

"They're not real," said Christiana. "Their existence is a myth."

"Like dragons," said Wendell, and ducked as Danny leaned over the seatback and swiped at him. "Seriously, though," the iguana said, straightening up, "there's a weird disease that rabbits get that makes 'em grow huge lumpy warty things on their heads. So maybe people saw those and made up stories about jackalopes."

"In which case they're not mythical, just gross," said Christiana.

"Says the girl who brought the *sheep brain* to class . . ."

"The sheep brain wasn't gross," said Christiana with dignity. "It was fascinating." She grinned suddenly. "And the fact that it grossed out most of the other girls was just a bonus."

Danny had to admit that Christiana was pretty cool . . . . when she wasn't telling him that dragons weren't real, that is.

The bus rumbled to a halt in the parking lot. Dust billowed around the campers as they unloaded.

"It's really dusty," said Spencer, coughing.

"Oh man, wait until we spend a day on a desert hike!" said Danny.

IT'S SO DUSTY YOUR SNOT TURNS BLACK.

OH GOODY, SOMETHING TO LOOK FORWARD TO...

The head counselor was a frog named Lenny, who wore a whistle and was wider than he was tall. He blew three short blasts on the whistle, then yelled, "Gather round, campers, gather round! Welcome to Camp Jackalope."

From past years, Danny knew that Lenny was a pretty good guy, although he believed in daily cabin inspections, which meant that campers had to spend a *whole twenty minutes* cleaning the cabin every morning and making sure the sleeping bags were neatly made. As far as Danny was concerned, there was a lot you could do with twenty minutes, including sleeping late and dropping a cherry bomb in a toilet, and it seemed criminal to waste it on making your bed.

The campers gathered round. "I see lots of familiar faces!" said Lenny cheerfully. "And lots of new friends! I'm so happy to welcome you all to summer camp!"

"He is, too," said Wendell under his breath. "*Really* excited. That's the disturbing part." Wendell was suspicious of anyone who was that cheerful *all the time*.

Lenny led them on a tour of Camp Jackalope, taking them to the camper cabins, showers, dining hall, lake, and the cabins for counselors. There were lots of trees everywhere.

"Can anybody tell me why there are trees, when we're in the desert?" asked Lenny.

Christiana, who had been looking bored, said, "Although this area is classified as high desert, we're at a high enough elevation that ponderosa pine forest is the dominant biome in areas sheltered by local topography."

"Errr," said Lenny, taken aback by a kid casually throwing around the words *biome* and *topography*. "Yes. That's exactly right!" He looked like he was about to pat Christiana on the head, then clearly thought better of it. "Once you get out of this little valley, though, it's all sagebrush and scrub and rocks." He shook a cheerful finger at Christiana.

"And scorpions, so don't forget to look where you put your hands, campers!"

Lenny waved toward several large buildings set back in the trees. "Those are off-limits," he said. "It's just where we keep the boxes of toilet paper and drain cleaner and the pumping equipment for the toilets and whatnot, so you're not missing much. If you need a grown-up and can't find one, go to the dining hall instead. There's always somebody there."

Danny couldn't remember anything being off-limits last year, and wondered if this had anything to do with the Bottle Rocket Incident.

"Now then," Lenny said, leading them back to the buses. "Your suitcases should be unloaded, so find your counselor for your cabin assignments!"

Cabin assignments were quick and easy. "Dragonbreath, Danny!" and "Elwood, Wendell!" were called in short order. Much to Danny's relief, he and Wendell were in the same cabin . . . and Spencer wasn't.

"Yes!" hissed Danny under his breath. He punched Wendell in the arm. Wendell punched him back.

Christiana was in one of the girls' cabins, of course. An extremely enthusiastic young alligator counselor came down to collect her.

Danny caught Spencer looking at him. He wondered if his cousin had seen him and Wendell punching each other, and felt a twinge of guilt. Then he remembered the last three levels of *Poison Sands,* where he had died and been *wa-waaaaah'd* at more than seventeen times. The guilt immediately disappeared.

The next few minutes were a whirl of unpacking, meeting the other guys in the cabin, and claiming bunks. (One of the nice things about Wendell was that he was always willing to take the bottom bunk.) When they went to dinner, Danny caught sight of Spencer across the room, at a table full of kids. He was talking nonstop to a small gecko who wore a glazed expression.

That was good. Clearly Spencer was fitting in fine, and more importantly, had found someone *else* to bother.

Girls sat with girls, and boys sat with boys, that being the immutable law of the universe, and since you ate with your cabin mates, it wasn't challenged here. Danny caught sight of Christiana with her snout on her hand, looking bored senseless.

"Poor Christiana," said Wendell.

"Maybe she'll sneak a sheep's brain into the cabin," said Danny.

When they went to the big campfire after dinner and got to toast marshmallows, Christiana broke ranks with the girls, stomped over, and plopped down next to them on their log.

I WISH I WAS AT SPACE CAMP.

"My counselor is named Heidi. She believes in better living through nail polish."

"Have a marshmallow," said Danny. "They're gonna tell ghost stories."

"I hate ghost stories," said Christiana, taking a marshmallow and stabbing it viciously with the wire skewer. "Instead of trying to collect data, everyone always winds up running away screaming. Most of these 'ghosts' are probably nothing more than garden-variety serial killers."

"You do remember last Halloween . . ."

"Vividly," said Christiana. "That's different. But there's no proof that, oh, the so-called ghostly hitchhiker, say, is anything but a person who knows about the story and has a twisted sense of humor. And the mental patient with hooks for hands isn't a ghost *at all.*"

"Oh give it a rest," said Danny. "They're starting."

"Not that long ago," said Bags, the assistant head counselor, "in a camp not very far from this one . . ."

It was a good story. Bags told it well. Then Lenny got up and told the one about the Ghost of the Bloody Finger, and then another counselor told the one about the Thing That Ran Across the Road.

AND IT MADE A RUSTLING SOUND, LIKE A SQUIRREL RUNNING OVER LEAVES, ONLY *MUCH HEAVIER*...

And when that was done, they sang the camp song "Hail to Thee, Camp Jackalope," which was admittedly not that great, but it was *tradition*.

43

Hail to thee, Camp Jackalope
Our home away from home
We won't get poison oak, we hope,
And never shall we roam.

There were twenty-seven verses, all in the same vein.

THIS SONG IS TERRIBLE. AND *LONG.*

I THINK LENNY MAKES UP THE VERSES IN HIS SPARE TIME.

Danny, aware that this was how nerds had fun, let it pass. As far as he was concerned, no matter how bad the song was, it was the start of a *great* summer camp.

A VERY WRONG TURN

In the middle of the night, Danny woke up and had to pee.

This was a more complicated process at camp than it was at home. At home, he just fell out of bed and staggered down the hallway to the bathroom, which had an ancient night-light with a happy daisy on it.*

*Danny had begged for a new night-light for years, preferably something with fangs and maybe lasers, but had so far been unsuccessful.

You could conduct the whole process without having to turn on the light or even wake up all the way.

At camp, however, you had to unzip the sleeping bag, climb down from the top bunk while trying not to step on Wendell's head, go outside the cabin, and walk down a path in the freezing cold. (Danny had been surprised, the first year, to learn that a desert is only hot during the day.) Instead of night-lights, there was a single uncovered yellow lightbulb by the boys' bathrooms, which had moths and beetles swarming around it in a fluttering horde. The bathrooms were also very cold, and there were more moths inside.

Still, Danny had been to Camp Jackalope twice before. He knew the drill. He navigated the moths, the cold, and the winding paths without a problem.

He did get a bit lost on the way back, though. One unmarked asphalt path looked a lot like another, and five of them converged on the bathrooms. Was his cabin at the end of that one? No, that was the cabin he'd been in last year. Was it by the big boulder?

He picked one that looked vaguely familiar and started down it. He'd gone about twenty yards when he realized that he was on the wrong path, but he continued, hoping that it would join up with the path leading back to his cabin.

It was awfully dark, but it didn't bother Danny. He'd been in haunted cellars and rat-infested sewers, which were *much* darker, and the stars over the desert were brighter and fiercer than anywhere else he'd ever been.

The path dead-ended at a building.

Danny blinked. It was one of the storage sheds, but surely the big Keep Out sign was new?

The Bottle Rocket Incident hadn't done *that* much damage. And Lenny had said that the storage sheds were just full of toilet paper and cleaning supplies. You didn't need a sign like that for toilet paper . . .

"Hey! Who's there?"

Danny jumped. A webbed hand landed on his shoulder.

"What are you doing out here, camper?" barked Lenny.

"Oh!" Danny was relieved to see it was only Lenny. "I got lost on the way back from the bathroom. How do I get back to Cabin Six?"

Lenny laughed. "Oh, is that all? Here, I'll walk you back."

Danny was a little embarrassed to have the frog walking with him like he was a little kid, but since the alternative was to keep blundering down paths and risk ending up at (horrors!) the girls' cabins, he fell in step with Lenny.

"Is that Keep Out sign new?" he asked.

IT'S NOTHING TO WORRY ABOUT.

HEALTH REGULATIONS.

"Oh," said Danny.

"Right," said Lenny. "Here's your cabin. Be more careful in the future." He turned and hurried off, nearly hopping.

Danny peered after him, puzzled, and wondered where a counselor could be going in such a hurry, when all the campers were supposed to be asleep.

The trouble didn't start until the third day.

They had had two full days of swimming, hiking, capture-the-flag, and extract-Wendell-from-the-mud-after-capture-the-flag . . .

It had been wonderful. There had even been crafts, and Danny had made most of a lanyard, an object so obviously useful that nobody could bring themselves to ask the counselors what the heck it was used for. Even the combined brain power of Wendell and Christiana couldn't figure it out.

Earl, the counselor in charge of crafts, was really excited about lanyards, though.

Really excited.

Spencer came over during lanyard making and watched over Danny's shoulder.

Then Spencer started talking about some other TV show and Danny considered feigning death, but then Earl came by to talk very seriously about code-bearing lanyards used during World War II and by the time he stopped, they were overdue for lunch.

After lunch was a trail ride. Trail rides were the very best part of Camp Jackalope. Danny loved horses, but he hardly ever got to ride one. He had begged his parents for a horse for two years, on the grounds that they could keep it in the back-yard, but they hadn't budged.

Crafts and s'mores and swimming you could get at almost any camp, but real horseback rides . . . that was something special. And Danny got to ride a horse named Bandit, which was an awesome name for a horse. He even got to groom Bandit after the ride.

Of course, there was a bit of a problem when both Danny and his horse decided that it would be a great time for a gallop. The horses behind

them suddenly shared this opinion, and there was a great deal of screaming from campers who had not previously been on top of a galloping horse and did not care for the experience.

Fortunately for Danny, the counselors all assumed that Bandit had run away with him. Since three campers had fallen off their horses and the reins of two others had become so hopelessly tangled that they had to bring one of the horses in backward, Danny felt it might be wise not to correct this impression.

It was midway through the third day when it occurred to Danny that he hadn't seen Spencer in a while. The younger dragon had been lurking around the shore during swimming in the morning, but now it was late afternoon, and Danny had gotten through both crafts and capture-the-flag without either awkward hero worship or a recap of the entire third season of *Vegetable Detectives.*

"I didn't see him at lunch either," offered Wendell. "I mean, not that I was looking . . ."

Danny didn't particularly *want* to see his cousin, but if Spencer had gotten into trouble, his mom was going to blame him. He was already on thin ice after the Bottle Rocket Incident, and if she took it in her head to clean his room while he was at camp, there were several things in there that she would probably be less than pleased about. (He'd *meant* to throw out that potato, but then it sprouted, and he was sort of curious as to what would happen . . .) Losing Spencer would make it a lot worse.

They had an hour of free time before dinner, and Christiana joined them outside the main lodge. She was wearing toenail polish and an expression of wounded dignity.

"The lanyard was bad enough, but this is too much," she said grimly. "I am being threatened with mascara. I am going to file a complaint, and then bite someone."

"We've got bigger troubles," said Danny. "Spencer's missing."

Christiana frowned. "Have you told a counselor?"

"Um. No." Danny was always loath to involve adults. "Should we?"

"Well, if you're sure he's—"

LOOK! OVER THERE!

Across the soccer field, emerging from the trees, was Spencer. He was looking around worriedly, as if afraid someone would notice him, and then he slunk along the edge of the trees until he reached the end of the field.

"Well, he's not dead," said Christiana.

"Good enough for me," said Danny, hopping off the porch. "Let's go see if the rope bridge is still there. I bet if we stand at the bottom and pull down on the middle, we can use it like a giant slingshot!"

"He looks like he's up to something," said Wendell, looking back over his shoulder.

"C'mon," said Danny. "He's *seven*. What could he possibly get up to?"

A MYTHICAL DISCOVERY

The next morning, Spencer wasn't at breakfast.

The head of his cabin came over to ask Danny if he'd seen his cousin.

"Um," said Danny. Spencer vanishing, even if they found him again, would be trouble, and letting Spencer get into trouble was going to bring the Wrath of Mom down on him. "I—uh—"

"He probably wasn't feeling well," said Wendell. "I bet he just went to the bathroom."

"He's a really pukey kid," said Danny, which was true. Spencer threw up a lot, sometimes in moving cars, sometimes just from the excitement of one of the TV shows he was describing.

The counselor grimaced. "If we can't find him—"

"We could go check on him," said Danny quickly. "We're done with breakfast."

Wendell was not actually done with breakfast, but sighed and put down his spoon. They hurried from the dining hall together.

"Do you know what that was?" asked Wendell sadly. "That was *frosted cereal*."

"So?"

BRAN.
THAT'S ALL MY
MOM BUYS. BRAN.
ENDLESS . . . ENDLESS
. . . BRAN.

"Oh," said Danny. "Hmm."

Wendell sighed again. "Oh, well . . . You think Spencer's really sick?"

"Probably not. But we should check."

No sooner had they come around the corner of the main lodge, though, than Danny grabbed Wendell's shoulder. "Hsst! Look!"

Spencer was sneaking out of the kitchen, hiding behind one of the Dumpsters. He was carrying something. Danny squinted.

"Is that . . . a bag of dinner rolls?"

"Looks like it."

"But where's he going?" asked Wendell. "And what does he want the bread for?"

"Maybe he's building a fort out of dinner rolls."

I'M NOT SURE IF ROLLS HAVE ENOUGH STRUCTURAL INTEGRITY—

Danny rolled his eyes. "Look, there's only one way to find out."

Spencer kept looking behind him, which made following him difficult, but he was also seven and rather slow, which helped. Danny and Wendell followed as he entered the woods.

Once under the trees, Spencer stopped checking behind him and started hurrying. The trees rapidly gave way to shrubs as he headed for one of the many canyons near Camp Jackalope, and began to descend the slope.

"Do you think he's running away?" Wendell asked.

Danny shrugged. Running away from an awesome camp and into the desert with only a bag of dinner rolls was pretty dumb, but

Spencer wasn't a rocket scientist. They probably wouldn't even let him *in* to space camp.

HE'D BE BETTER OFF WITH WATER. EVEN I KNOW THAT.

They started down the rocky slope after him. There were no trees at the bottom, and Danny spotted a couple of honest-to-goodness cactus. It was genuine desert down there.

At the bottom of the canyon, Spencer suddenly stopped and looked behind him.

"Oops," said Wendell.

Spencer's eyes went wide, and he started to run.

Pebbles bounced and slid around them as they ran down the slope. Wendell missed a step, nearly fell, caught himself, and slid dustily to the bottom, yelling.

SPENCER, WAIT!

Spencer was running down the canyon. It was a dry wash, an old streambed that only had water when it rained. The dirt was packed hard, and Danny was pretty sure he could catch up to Spencer eventually—if one of them didn't step in a hole or trip on a rock first.

"Spencer, wait! What's wrong? What are you doing?" Danny wished his mother could see him, being responsible and everything. She'd better appreciate it later. The next time he needed a new video game, for example.

Danny was gaining. He could hear Wendell panting behind him.

"Spencer—"

The little dragon suddenly cut sharply to one side. There was a shallow cave there, barely more than a depression under a shelf of rock. Danny skidded to a halt as Spencer dove into the cave.

"Go away!" his cousin yelled. "Go away! I won't let you hurt him!"

"Hurt *who*?" asked Danny, approaching the cave.

"Go *away!*"

Wendell trotted up, wheezing. "What's he— pant, pant—talking about?"

Danny took a step forward and leaned down to look into the cave.

Spencer was crouched under the rock shelf with his arm around something.

Something *alive.*

Something that Danny recognized immediately, but had never expected to see.

IT'S A DRAGON THING

Danny was not particularly surprised by the fact that jackalopes really existed. Being a dragon himself, he had firsthand experience with legendary things lurking around the edges of everyday life.

Wendell needed a minute.

"That's a jackalope!" he said. "But they're mythic—"

He stopped.

He looked at Danny.

He tried again. "But they're impossib—"

He stopped.

He looked at Spencer.

THEY'RE . . . NOT VERY LIKELY?

Danny thought the whole question of whether they existed or not was stupid, since the jackalope was clearly sitting *right there,* so he skipped to the important part.

"How did you *find* one?" he asked Spencer.

Spencer hunched his shoulders. "He found *me.* And you're not gonna take him away!"

"Relax," said Danny, sitting down on a rock, "nobody's gonna take anybody away."

"Well. . . ." Spencer looked at the jackalope. The jackalope looked at Spencer. It had big liquid eyes, like a Japanese anime princess. It put a paw on his arm, and the little dragon nodded.

"Nobody in my cabin would talk to me. They were all bigger and they just pretended I didn't exist. And you didn't want to hang out with me either, and I had *nobody* to talk to, and I didn't want to be here *anyway*. I don't even *like* horses."

"So I came out here," said Spencer. "I mean, I went for a walk, because I wanted to—to be alone—" He gulped a little.

Wendell knew perfectly well that meant that Spencer wanted to have a good cry in private, but it didn't seem diplomatic to say so.

Danny, who thought "diplomacy" was that thing you got when you graduated from high school, opened his mouth to say "Were you crying?" and then closed it again because Wendell was punching him in the arm.

"Err. Right. Yes," he said instead.

"And then I looked up, and there was Jack." It—he—was undeniably a jackalope. He had two short little prongy horns and a white band of fur around his neck.

"I dunno," said Wendell. "But if it's just a regular rabbit with that disease that makes it grow weird tumors, the tumors are awfully symmetrical. And he's a lot bigger than any rabbit I've ever seen."

Danny nodded. He was thinking something similar—minus words like *symmetrical*—but it was good to have Nerd Confirmation.

"He's really nice," said Spencer defensively. "And he's in trouble."

TROUBLE?

"Something happened to his whole family," said Spencer. "All the other jackalopes too. He's really scared."

"Does he *talk*?" asked Wendell, baffled.

The jackalope opened his mouth. Wendell and Danny leaned forward, fascinated.

GRA-HOOONK!

"He sort of gronks," said Spencer. "But that's not it. He—we kinda—look, I just *know,* okay?"

"Some kind of jackalope telepathy?" asked Wendell skeptically.

"I knew you wouldn't believe me," said Spencer, wrapping his arms around his knees and looking stubborn in the way that only an angry seven-year-old can. "But it's *true.*"

Danny had no problem believing that Spencer could talk to the jackalope. He himself had had excellent conversations with rats and sentient potato salad, despite the lack of a common language between them. You just had to listen the right way.

No, Danny's problem was that of all the people a jackalope could choose to talk to, why *Spencer*? Seriously? Danny would have been delighted to talk to a jackalope, and he had to admit that he was feeling just a tiny bit jealous of his cousin.

He stifled a sigh. Oh well. Maybe the jackalope liked hearing about TV shows he hadn't seen. Clearly there were more important issues at stake.

"Does he know what's happened to his family?"

Spencer shook his head. "He's not sure. He was hiding too, and when he finally came back home, they were gone. And lots of other jackalopes have been vanishing too."

"Could they have gotten sick? Or gotten rabies? Rabies can go through a population like crazy." He gave Jack a wary look, as if expecting him to start foaming at the mouth at any moment.

"He doesn't think they're dead," said Spencer. Jack stamped a hind leg, as if for emphasis. "He hasn't smelled blood or anything. There's something else going on. I think something's kidnapping them."

"Yeesh," said Wendell.

Jack nodded so hard his ears flapped.

"I think he's the only one left," said Spencer somberly.

"Should we tell the counselors?" asked Wendell. "I mean, taking jackalopes has to be illegal. I'm sure they're an endangered species, being mythical and all."

Danny and Spencer exchanged glances. When you're a dragon, you get a lot of firsthand experience in people not believing you exist.

"They wouldn't believe us," said Spencer.

Danny hated to agree with Spencer about anything, but the kid was right. "Yeah. They'd think he was one of those rabbits with the tumors, or they'd want to dissect him or something. You can't trust most grown-ups with stuff like this."

"Look," said Wendell, "regardless, we have to get back to camp. They're gonna come looking for us."

"He's right," said Danny. "We're supposed to be checking on you in the bathroom right now, and we've already taken waaaaay too long for that."

Spencer turned to Jack and held out his hands. "Are you gonna be okay? You'll stay hidden, right? I brought you food, and we'll come back as soon as we can."

Jack peered warily out at the desert, then turned back to Spencer and put his paws on the dragon's knee. He rubbed his head briefly against Spencer's cheek, then retreated to the back of the cave and picked up a roll.

"Don't worry," said Danny, not sure if he was talking to Spencer or Jack. "We'll figure out what to do. We always come up with *something*."

Wendell rolled his eyes. He knew better than anybody else that "something" usually involved dangling over volcano pits or almost being eaten by giant squid.

"Don't give me that look, Wendell. We totally do."

"Uh-huh."

"It'll work out."

"Sure."

"Nobody ever *dies,* anyway."

Wendell was forced to concede the point.

When they walked out of the forest, the counselor for Spencer's cabin spotted them immediately. "Danny! Spencer! I checked the bathroom, but you weren't there, and I was getting ready to send out search parties!"

"Uh," said Danny. "He's fine now. He just—uh—"

"He needed some fresh air," said Wendell hurriedly. "So we went for a little walk. He feels better now, right, Spencer?"

"Right," said Spencer. "Loads better. I thought I was gonna puke up all that oatmeal I ate before. My stomach was all gurgly and I was all like this—"

"Well, okay . . ." said the counselor. "Do you need to go to the nurse? You probably should—"

"I'm fine now," said Spencer. "If I start to feel sick again, I'll go."

"As long as you're sure." The counselor gave them one last suspicious look, then turned back to the game of dodge ball he was orchestrating.

"Well," said Wendell. "That was close. Now what?"

Danny was of the opinion that the only thing better than one nerd brain working on a problem was *two* nerd brains on the problem.

"Let's tell Christiana. Maybe she'll have an idea."

The crested lizard was more than willing to join them, since her cabin mates and counselor Heidi were threatening her with something called a "makeover." Danny hurriedly outlined the situation.

"But jackalopes aren't—"

"*Don't* say they're not real," said Danny. "It doesn't matter, okay? We'll show you a jackalope later. Just pretend for the moment that we're not nuts and use that huge brain to figure out what we ought to do."

Christiana gave him a dubious look and opened her mouth to say something—he just *knew* it was going to be something sarcastic—but then she took a deep breath and said, "Okay. For the sake of argument, then," and put her head together with Wendell's.

Danny attempted to help, but after both of his best ideas were shot down in rapid succession, on the grounds that they did not have access to either a hang glider or fifty live chickens, he and Spencer eventually wound up playing wall-bounce with a tennis ball.

After about ten minutes the nerds presented their findings.

To Danny's surprise, Christiana immediately dismissed the idea of going to the counselors. "Assuming they believed us, which they won't, they'd have to get the Forest Service involved. They're the people who deal with poachers. And they're totally overworked, so it'd be weeks before anybody came out, and your hypothetical jackalope buddy would be hypothetically dead by the time they got here."

Spencer gulped.

"It'll be okay," said Danny, patting him on the shoulder. "We'll take care of it." He felt a little weird saying that to Spencer—*Spencer!*—but the look of relief that the younger dragon gave him reminded him uncomfortably of his mother saying "He's crazy about you."

"We need to find out who's responsible before we can do anything," said Christiana. "And I want to get a good look at the beast too. I've got some questions."

"His name's Jack," said Spencer sullenly. "And he's not hypuh—hyp—hypuhntheticall."

Christiana waved this off as unimportant. Wendell jumped in.

"There's a scavenger hunt this evening. We're all supposed to be out looking for—oh, giant pinecones and heart-shaped rocks and things. So if we can all slip away from our groups and meet out in the woods, we can go back to the canyon. Nobody'll miss us for at least an hour, and if they do find us, we'll just say we're looking for something on the scavenger list."

Danny was about to rail against an unjust universe that had not adapted sharks to desert life, but Spencer broke in. "Okay. I'll meet you guys here. But you promise you won't tell anybody about Jack?"

"Geez, Spencer, of course not," said Danny.

"Definitely not," said Wendell.

"I'll need to see him before I believe he's a jackalope," said Christiana. "But I'm a skeptic, not a rat."

And with that, Spencer had to be satisfied.

SCAVENGING FOR JACKALOPES

It was a really cool scavenger hunt, and Danny was sorry to miss it. Everybody had flashlights for when it got really dark, and the cabin that found the most items on the list got candy bars. In a perfect world, the scavenger hunt would have included things like "severed heads" and "cowboy treasure," but Danny was always willing to improvise.

Still, some things were more important.

"We'll hunt for the giant pinecone," he told their cabin leader, and he and Wendell peeled off from the rest of the group.

"Don't go too far!" the counselor called after them as they vanished into the trees.

"We won't!" Wendell called back. Being Wendell, he managed to sound trustworthy and responsible.*

"Where's Spencer?" asked Wendell when they got near the top of the canyon.

"I don't know, he's supposed to be around here somewhere—"

"I'm over here!" Spencer peeked out from behind a bush. "Did anybody follow you?"

"Listen, kid," said Danny, "I have been sneaking around grown-ups since you were wearing diapers. Did anybody follow *you*?"

"No." Spencer dusted pine needles off his tail. "Where's your girlfriend?"

"Who, Christiana?" Danny snorted. "She's not *my* girlfriend."

"Whoa, don't look at me." Wendell put up his hands. "Anyway, she says marriage is a bourgeois institution designed to oppress women."

*Danny wished he could sound like that, but whenever he tried, his mother immediately said, "What are you up to?!" and put him under twenty-four-hour surveillance.

93

"A bor . . . borjz . . . awuh?"

"I'm not sure either," admitted Wendell, "but she gets really mad talking about it, so I figured I'd stop asking."

This struck Danny as sensible. Christiana might not believe in stuff like ghosts or UFOs, but she believed very strongly and loudly in things like "green energy" and "social justice." (He had been a bit disappointed to learn that social justice did not involve dressing up like a superhero and fighting crime.)

They sat and waited.

Christiana didn't show up.

"Do you think she went to a counselor and ratted us out?" asked Spencer.

NO!

"She wouldn't do that," said Danny. "She's weird, but she's on our side."

They waited some more. It was getting too dark to see without flashlights, but Danny was reluctant to turn his on, for fear that other campers would see the lights.

"Maybe we should go without her," said Spencer.

"I'm sure she'll turn up," said Wendell, shoving his glasses farther up his snout.

And she did indeed turn up—out of breath, and looking very annoyed. "Come on," she panted, "let's get out of here."

"What happened to you?" asked Wendell.

THAT STUPID FROG LENNY.

"I ran into him on the way here, and he wanted to know where I was going. He was super-nosy." She scowled. "I dunno what got into him, but he was all suspicious. 'Your cabin all went over there, camper! Better go catch up with them!' I had to tell him that Heidi chipped a nail and sent me back to the cabin to get more polish."

"Huh," said Danny. "You know, he acted a little weird the other night too. I got lost getting back to the cabin and wound up near the off-limits buildings, and he showed up."

"After the Bottle Rocket Incident last year, I'd be suspicious too," said Wendell drily. "He probably thought you were trying to set the whole place on fire. Again."

IT WAS AN ACCIDENT!

"Bottle Rocket Incident?" asked Spencer.

"Uh—"

"Later, okay?" said Christiana. "I don't want to be here if Lenny shows up again."

"Right, right." Danny scrambled to his feet and they hurried down the slope toward the canyon.

Jack was nowhere to be seen at first, but then Spencer whistled. A moment later, Jack emerged from behind a cactus and immediately hid behind Spencer.

Christiana said, "Huh!" which from her was an admission of profound astonishment.

"Christiana, meet Jack. Jack, Christiana," said Danny.

Jack poked his nose warily around Spencer.

Christiana dropped to her knees in the middle of the sand and held out a hand. Jack looked at Spencer, then slowly approached her, like a dog that wants to be friendly but isn't sure that it isn't going to get kicked.

"There's a good jackalope," said Christiana. "I won't hurt you."

Jack sniffed her fingers and allowed himself to be petted behind the ears.

Danny tried not to seethe with jealousy. *He* hadn't gotten to pet the jackalope yet.

"May I?" asked Christiana, tapping Jack's antlers. Jack made a gronky noise.

"He says yes," said Spencer.

Christiana ran a hand over the jackalope's antlers, tapped one with a claw-tip, said, "Hmm."

"I don't think they're tumors," said Wendell.

"Good jackalope." She stood up again. Jack scampered back to lurk behind Spencer's legs.

She looked at Wendell. Wendell nodded.

"What?" said Danny. "That's *it*? It took hours and a manif—manifest—the ghost had to actually appear before you believed in it, and you look at the jackalope for five minutes and call it a new species?"

"There's plenty of precedent for new species," said Christiana, unruffled. "They found a new yak in Asia a few years ago, and that's way bigger than Jack here. And the latest *Scientific Reptilian* had an article about possible survivals of giant false vampire bats in Mexico—"

LA LA LA
I CAN'T HEAR
YOU

(Wendell had stopped having nightmares, but was not yet prepared to talk rationally about the giant false vampire bats.)

"I suppose you believe in Bigfoot, then," said Danny. He couldn't believe they'd brought the Junior Skeptic around without a fight.

"Don't be ridiculous," said Christiana. "A dinosaur with gigantic feet surviving in a heavily traveled area like the Pacific Northwest? Somebody would have hit one with a car by now. But this is pretty remote, and people don't hike in the desert nearly as much as they hike in the woods. A creature the size of Jack, who looks more or less like a rabbit at a casual glance?" She shrugged. "I'm willing to keep an open mind."

"That's a first," Danny started to mutter, but Wendell kicked him in the shins.

DOES THAT MEAN YOU'LL HELP US FIND OUT WHO'S HUNTING JACK?

WELL, DUH. I'M A SKEPTIC, NOT A JERK.

"Oh, good," said Spencer. He hugged Jack. "This'll be awesome! It'll be just like the third season of *Quadro Force,* when the Black Samurai comes back but they've got a new pilot and they have to protect the planet of Mamarkand from—"

"Quiet!" hissed Wendell.

Spencer blinked. Danny was a little surprised too—sure, he usually wanted to tell Spencer to be quiet, but Wendell wasn't usually the type to snap—and then he heard it too.

Voices.

Coming this way.

"Oh no," whispered Danny, "somebody found us!"

GRONK!

"I dunno, boss," said one voice, shockingly close, "I haven't seen any of those horned bunnies in a while."

"Shut up," said another voice. "I've seen at least one more out here."

Spencer looked around wildly, perhaps preparing to make a break for it, but Danny grabbed his arm.

The older kids exchanged glances. Three things were immediately obvious.

One, some freak echo had brought the voices to them from up the canyon.

Two, the owners of the voices were between them and the woods.

Three, the second voice belonged to head counselor Lenny.

"It's him!" hissed Wendell. "He's the one doing it! I knew it! I knew nobody that cheerful could be up to any good!"

"Never mind that!" Christiana shot back. *"Hide!"*

It had never before occurred to Danny just how few places there were to hide in the desert. Saguaro cactus were really impressive-looking, but they weren't wide enough to hide behind, and all the scrubby little bushes were dried out and thin and you could see right through them.

"The cave," he said, grabbing Spencer by the back of the shirt and shoving him into it.

"Ow!"

"Get in there!" Danny wiggled in after. "You too, Jack!"

Cave was probably being too kind. It was a shelf of rock that extended barely to Danny's waist. It was a little taller in the back, but not by much.

"We can't possibly all fit—" Wendell began.

"I don't think—" Christiana started to say.

Crunch-crunch-crunch came the sound of footsteps on sand.

"Really, boss, is it worth wandering around here all night looking for one more bunny?"

Christiana and Wendell dove into the hole.

Wendell would have sworn that there was no way to fit four kids and a jackalope into the cave, and he was very nearly right. Somebody's elbow was in his ribs and somebody had a knee practically in his throat and he could hear Spencer whispering "There's a foot in my face! Stop it, *stop it!*" and Danny was trying to get his tail out from under Christiana and Jack's antlers were hitting Wendell in the glasses with a tiny *tick-tick-tick* noise.

"Everybody, *quiet!*" Danny whispered as loudly as he dared.

For a wonder, everybody was.

Even their breathing sounded horribly loud in Danny's ears. Surely Lenny would hear them, or see somebody's tail sticking out or somebody would sneeze . . .

"*Yes,* it's worth it for one more bunny," snapped Lenny. He was definitely close now, not just echoing down the canyon. "Do you *know* what some people will pay for powdered jackalope horn?"

"I still don't get what they're using it for," said the other speaker.

Feet came into view. One set was big and webbed, and the other was stumpy and scaled. Danny thought maybe they belonged to Earl, the counselor in charge of crafts. Apparently lanyards had not been his greatest interest in life after all.

"It doesn't matter what they're using it for," said Lenny, annoyed. "I don't care if they're sprinkling it on cupcakes! It's selling for nearly eight hundred dollars an ounce!"

"Those'd be really expensive cupcakes," said Earl.

"You're an idiot," said Lenny.

"Aw, boss, that's not nice . . ."

They were right outside the cave.

"Keep your eyes peeled," ordered Lenny. "They're getting a lot harder to catch these days. If this is the last shipment, I want it to be a big one."

They're going to see us, Danny thought, *they* have *to see us, what am I going to do, we can't let them take Jack, but if I breathe fire on a counselor I am going to get* into *so much* trouble—

Lenny and Earl didn't see them. The rock ledge might have been waist-high on Danny, but it was only a little over knee-high on a grown-up, and the shadows under it were very deep. Lenny glanced down, saw nothing of interest, and kept walking.

They were nearly past the cave now. Danny listened to the *crunch-crunch-crunch* going away and dared to hope that he would not be spending his life in prison for attempted counselorcide.

Danny made another desperate tug at his tail and poked Christiana in a tender spot. She jerked, clipping Wendell in the back of the head with her knee. He tried not to yelp, but his chin hit the sand with a muffled *thump*.

The footsteps stopped.

"Did you hear somethin'?" asked Earl.

"Probably just a ground squirrel," said Lenny. "Jackalopes go *gronk!* and run away, they don't thump around."

The crunching started up again and faded into the night. Crickets began to chirp from the woods.

"I think it's clear," whispered Wendell, when

he absolutely could not stand the thought of having Christiana's knee smooshing the back of his neck for a second longer.

They crawled and rolled and staggered out of the cave. Danny had rock patterns imprinted on his cheek, and Spencer was whining about how somebody had been crushing his arm.

"Now what?" asked Christiana.

"We've got to get out of here," said Danny. "They might come back this way."

". . . bruises hurt for *days* and they turn *purple* . . ."

"If we go into the woods, we've got a lot more places to hide," said Wendell.

They hurried up the slope toward the woods.

". . . I bet I won't be able to catch or write or do crafts or *anything* . . ."

"Look," said Danny, exasperated, "fine, you got a bruise, big deal! Would you rather let Lenny have Jack?"

Spencer glared at the ground and mumbled something that might have been "No."

"We've got to figure something out," said Danny. "We can't let him catch Jack."

"And we've only got three more *days,*" said Spencer.

"First we need to figure out what Lenny's done with the other jackalopes," said Christiana. "If they're nearby, that's good. If he's got them somewhere else . . ."

She stopped, because there really wasn't much she could say. If they couldn't find the missing jackalopes, they'd have to find a grown-up who could help them, and what grown-up would possibly believe a story about jackalope smuggling?

"Jack could come home with me," said Spencer. "He'd be safe there."

There was an awkward silence.

"C'mon, Spencer," said Danny, "you've seen all those dorky movies about people with wild animals. They always go back to the wild at the end of the movie."

YOU CAN'T REALLY KEEP WILD ANIMALS AS PETS.

"I could," said Spencer. "Jack's different. He's nice."

Danny sighed. "Your mom won't let you have a *cat,*" he said finally. "Or a dog. She has allergies, remember? When we tried to do Easter at Aunt Isabel's house, she made that big scene with the nose drops and accused Isabel of trying to poison her because there was a cat hair in her mashed potatoes?"

Spencer clearly *did* remember, because his shoulders sagged. (In fairness, no one in Danny's family would ever forget that Easter, which had been extremely dramatic, and Danny's mom had spent most of dinner trying to mediate between her sisters Shirley and Isabel, who were Not Speaking to Each Other, Thank You. On the drive home, Danny's father had threatened to *really* poison the mashed potatoes next time, and Danny's mom had said, "Oh honey, don't tempt me!" and had giggled hysterically for the next forty miles.)

"Besides, we want to save Jack's family too," said Wendell. "He'd be sad without his family. And that means we have to stop Lenny."

"That's great in theory," said Christiana, "but how do we actually stop a grown-up? Remember, we've only got three more days."

"You should just breathe fire on him," said Spencer.

"First of all," said Danny, rubbing his snout, "you can't just go breathing fire on people. You get in serious trouble. And secondly . . . I'm not very good at breathing fire."

Christiana did not say anything, but she was so obviously Not Saying Anything that Danny kind of wished she'd just make fun of him and get it over with.

Spencer stared at him. "You can't breathe fire?"

"Not very well," Danny admitted. "I mean, I've *done* it, but it has to be really cold or I have to be really scared. I'm not good at it." He avoided Spencer's eyes.

YES, WELL . . .

"He's done it when it mattered," said Wendell loyally.

"But cousin Oscar can breathe fire, and he's younger than you!"

"Let's assume that setting fire to Lenny is off the table," said Wendell. "Or stringing him up or keel-hauling him or anything else like that. You can't *do* that to grown-ups. They put you in a Home for Troubled Youth or military school or something."

Danny had been threatened with military school often enough in his life that he thought Wendell was probably right, although he had only a hazy impression of what they did to you there—made you polish potatoes or peel shoes or something.

"Anyway, the important thing is to save Jack's family," said Christiana. "Once we've rescued them, we can work something out. We can send letters to the authorities. They don't need to know we're kids." (Danny suspected that if Christiana and Wendell were writing the letters, nobody would even *suspect* they were kids. Wendell actually had his own letterhead.)

"Fiiiiine," said Spencer, drawing out the word with a long sigh. "So how do we do that?"

"We'll have to get more information," said Christiana. "And that means somebody has to follow Lenny."

"I'll do it," said Danny. "I'm totally sneaky!"

Wendell looked dubious, but since the iguana sounded like a bull moose wearing clogs when he tried to sneak anywhere, he didn't say anything.

"Right now we have to get back," said Christiana. "The scavenger hunt's got to be over soon, and people are going to wonder where we are."

"Jack? Can you stay out of Lenny's way?" asked Spencer worriedly.

"Gronk!" said Jack, and saluted.

And with that, the jackalope disappeared into the night, and the four kids trudged back to camp.

TRAILING THE FROG

Danny was in his element.

If you wanted long division solved or if you had to know the average yearly rainfall in Death Valley, you asked a nerd. But if you wanted bad guys shadowed, the best possible person to ask was Danny Dragonbreath.

Hadn't he helped foil the horribly sneaky ninja frogs of mythical Japan? Had he not slain the alpha were-wiener with a silver toasting fork?

Yes. He was definitely the person for the job.

The fact that Lenny the frog was not cooperating by doing anything notably suspicious didn't matter at all.

HE SLUNK . . .

. . . AND HE SKULKED.

HE TRIED NOT TO LET THE
BIG FROG OUT OF HIS SIGHT.

Unfortunately Lenny did nothing more diabolical than organize a game of dodge ball, which *was* indeed pretty diabolical, particularly for Wendell, but probably not related to the jackalopes.

THWUNG!

By late afternoon, Danny was starting to get discouraged. He hadn't seen Lenny do *anything* bad, and they only had two days left. He could feel the clock ticking over his shoulder, and if time ran out, there would be no one to help Jack's family.

Wendell and Christiana were covering for him with the counselors, claiming he was in the bathroom or had just gone over there behind that rock, or that they'd just seen him in the big lodge. But they couldn't keep it up forever. He'd already had to stop watching for two hours of horseback riding, and his enjoyment of riding Bandit was largely eclipsed by worrying what Lenny might be up to behind his back.

What was he going to do?

Then, late in the day, Danny got his break.

"Great," said Lenny to a little knot of grownups, while Danny lurked in the bushes. "Time to get ready for campfire, while the campers are eating dinner. You three go get the marshmallows, and Bob, you start the bonfire now so we've got some good coals when it's time to roast."

The group split, but Lenny himself stayed in the middle of the path, rocking back and forth on his big webbed feet. Behind the bush, Danny's eyes narrowed. Then the big frog turned and made his way up the path, toward the off-limits cabins.

Danny kept pace, slinking from tree to tree, trying to stay out of sight. Lenny vanished into his cabin, but came out again almost immediately, carrying something.

Lenny turned down the path to the cabin with the big Keep Out sign. As Danny watched from behind a pine tree, Lenny put down what he was holding—it looked like a toolkit—and pulled out a length of chain and a very big padlock.

I knew they wouldn't put up a Keep Out sign for toilet paper! Danny thought.

The big frog finished pad-locking the door and stepped back to admire his handiwork. "There!" he said, sounding satisfied. "That should keep anybody from tripping over the merchandise."

The head counselor turned—Danny quickly pulled his head back behind the tree—and strolled down the pathway, whistling the camp song. Danny waited until he was gone, then hurried off to tell his partners in crime.

"We've got to get into that cabin!" said Spencer.

"Maybe we could go tomorrow—" Wendell began.

"Tonight," said Danny firmly. "We don't have that much time."

Christiana was staring off into the distance, the way she did when she was thinking very hard. Finally she said, "Lenny's always at campfire. He likes to make sure they sing all fifty million verses of the camp song. They're doing s'mores tonight, and that always takes forever, and somebody always burns themselves on the chocolate or pokes themselves in the eye with a marshmallow. Tonight would be the best time."

"It *would* have to be s'more night," muttered Spencer. "I wanted a s'more."

YOU
AND ME
BOTH.

Wendell's mother had made a health-food s'more once with carob and gluten-free graham crackers. The iguana still had nightmares.

"You can still back out," said Danny.

"No, I can't. It's for Jack." Spencer pulled himself up as tall as he could, which wasn't very. "What do we do?"

Danny had already made a plan, and one he thought was worthy of a nerd.

"We'll go as soon as they hand out the marshmallows. Christiana, you be the guard. Lenny should be tied up at campfire, but Earl isn't. Spencer, can you stop him?"

Spencer grinned. "Leave him to me."

A few minutes later, after they had gulped their

marshmallows cold, they slunk through the trees toward their goal. As they passed the crafts cabin, Danny heard Spencer's voice in the distance.

"So then the three alien detectives get this case, right . . ."

"Uh-huh?" Counselor Earl did not sound at all interested. "That's fascinating, but—"

"No, you *have* to hear this bit, this is where it really gets *good*—"

Danny grinned. Spencer had finally found a way to use his one talent for good.

The trio reached the forbidden cabins. Christiana took up a post behind a large bush. "Okay. If anybody's coming, I'll call like a great horned owl."

"You can do that?" asked Danny.

"Well, of course," said Christiana, looking vaguely offended. "What? You can't?"

Of all the things Danny could do with his time, sitting around practicing owl calls had somehow never occurred to him.

"*I* can do owl calls," said Wendell.

"Of course you can," muttered Danny.

They eventually settled on a mockingbird imitating a barred owl, which sounded no different from any of the other calls to Danny but seemed to make them both happy.

There was still a big padlock on the door, in addition to the Keep Out sign. But once again, Danny thought, Lenny was thinking like a grown-up, not like a kid.

Wendell saw it too.

Somebody Lenny's size would never have been able to fit through, but for Danny it was easy. The only hard part was actually reaching the window.

OOF! DID YOU REALLY NEED THAT SEVENTEENTH MARSHMALLOW?

Once Danny was inside, it was an easy matter to get his feet on a table that had been shoved under the window. It was very dark in the cabin and it smelled like the zoo.

"I think this is the right place!" he said.

"Great!" said Wendell. "Pull me up!"

This was somewhat harder—Wendell had never in his life managed to do a pull-up in PE, and generally just hung off the bar looking miserable until the coach took pity on him and let him get down. But Danny finally hauled him up through the window and into the cabin.

It was very dark. Something banged on something else with a wiry metal sound. Danny could hear breathing and in the gloom there was a suggestion of eyes.

"Please let it be jackalopes," whispered Wendell, "please let it be jackalopes."

"What else *could* it be?" Danny whispered back.

MAYBE LENNY'S TRADING ILLEGALLY IN TIGERS.

I DON'T THINK THERE ARE TIGERS IN THE DESERT...

THERE AREN'T SUPPOSED TO BE JACKALOPES EITHER!

Danny felt his way along the wall until he came to a light switch and turned it on.

"There," said Danny, "now we can see what we're—"

He turned.

Wendell said, ". . . Oh."

BUNNY STAMPEDE

Danny had been hoping to find Jack's family. He hadn't really thought about how many there would be—his mom and dad, maybe a couple of brothers and sisters or a spare aunt or two.

There were *dozens*. Maybe hundreds. There were

cages stacked on the tables and under the tables and in corners, and every single one was full of jackalopes staring at him with big dark eyes.

"Crapmonkeys," said Danny, which his mother sometimes said while driving.

"Jack must have a really big family," said Wendell weakly.

The jackalopes watched them. They seemed to

be all ages, from big males with antlers twice as big as Jack's to tiny little jackalope kits with little bumps where their horns would grow in. But all of them looked terribly sad.

"It'll be okay," said Danny, hooking his fingers around the bars of the nearest cage. "We're here to help."

The jackalopes in the cage huddled at the far end, looking frightened. Danny was starting to think that breathing fire on Lenny might be worth it after all.

"We'll get you out," said Wendell. "We're friends of Jack's."

They waited. The jackalopes rustled and thumped in their cages. One made a pathetic gronking sound, and was quickly hushed by the others.

"I don't think they understand," said Wendell sadly.

And then Danny said something he never, ever expected to say in his life.

The latches on the cages were easy. Wendell started on one side and Danny started on the other.

"You know . . ." called Wendell, "I have a bad thought."

Danny sighed.

"There's still the padlock on the door. We can't get through it from this side either."

"Maybe we can boost them out of the window," said Danny. He looked at the animals in the cages and frowned. It didn't seem likely that the jackalopes would want to be picked up, but he wasn't sure how else to do it.

"They seem so *depressed*," said Wendell gloomily.

"My cousin Steve says that captivity is really hard on some animals," said Danny, flipping more cage latches. "You can't keep them as pets or in zoos or anything. They just pine away."

As the doors of the cages opened, one jackalope, bolder than the rest, poked its head out.

"That's it!" said Danny excitedly. "Freedom! C'mon, you can do it!"

He started down the next row of cages.

His hand had just closed over the first latch when he heard a sound that he'd been dreading.

Somewhere nearby, an owl was hooting.

"Wendell! Wendell, we have a problem!"

"Tell me about it!" The iguana had caught his fingers on the drop bar of the last cage and stuck one in his mouth. "That stings!"

"No, doofus, there was hooting! It's Christiana! *Somebody's coming!*"

"Are you sure? That sounded like more of a boreal owl than a mockingbird imitating a barred—"

Danny grabbed Wendell by the collar and stuffed him under the table.

"I'm just sayin'," muttered Wendell.

He dove under the table after his friend.

"The light!" said Wendell. "They'll see the light!"

"They've seen it already, if they're that close!"

They crouched down behind the line of cages. Outside, someone fumbled with the padlock. One of the jackalopes looked down at them with interest.

The door opened.

"You left the light on, idiot," said Lenny over his shoulder. "It's wasting electricity. Do you think we're made of money?"

"Sorry, boss," said Earl. "I meant to check, but one of the campers had to talk to me. Forever. Something about a show with zebra smugglers and a prophecy and I don't know what-all. I may need to get the DVD."

"Yeah, yeah . . ." Lenny glanced over the cages. "I guess this is a big enough load. Wish we'd been able to catch the last couple, though."

"What are you going to do after this?" asked Earl.

"Saguaro cactus probably," said Lenny. "Landscapers'll pay a pretty penny for a full-grown saguaro."

Next to Danny, Wendell squirmed with outrage. "That's illegal!" he hissed in Danny's ear. "They take like three hundred years to grow! You're not supposed to dig them up!"

"This is *not the time,* Wendell!"

Lenny looked at his watch. "Buyers should be here in an hour. The campers ought to be in bed by then."

An hour! Danny's heart sank. They had to do something right now! If only Lenny would leave—and leave without noticing that the cages were unlatched and ajar, that one in the back was actually wide open, and oh god, a jackalope was *sticking its head out of it*—

WHY COULDN'T YOU HAVE STAYED SCARED A LITTLE LONGER?

"Boss!" said Earl. "Look, one's getting loose!"

"Catch him!" Lenny moved down the aisle toward the open cage door. If he reached it, he'd be less than a foot from where Danny and Wendell were crouched, and he would absolutely spot them.

Danny did the only thing he could think of to do. He jumped to his feet, slammed his shoulder into the table, and yelled, "The doors are open! RUN!"

It worked. Hitting the table knocked most of the cage doors wide open, and the jackalopes—panicked.

It was not a very large space.

There were a *lot* of jackalopes.

"STAMPEDE!" screamed Wendell, and then a jackalope launched itself off his head, knocking his glasses to the ground.

Lenny grabbed for them as they passed, but the jackalopes moved like hairy lightning. They ran between his legs and past his knees, they launched off the table and over his head. It was like being in a room full of bouncy balls with antlers.

They poured out of the building. Danny frantically threw latches open on the remaining cages.
There was only one row left when he felt a hand
close over the back of his shirt.

"I've got the other one, boss!" said Earl, who had Wendell in a headlock, although since Wendell had lost his glasses and couldn't have found his way out of a paper sack, this was hardly necessary.

The frog looked down at Danny and said, "*Dragonbreath*. I might have *known*."

"What do we do with 'em, boss?" asked Earl.

Lenny sighed. "Look, Danny, Wendell, I know you think you've seen something strange here, but I assure you, you're mistaken. We're collecting specimens for the zoo—"

"You are NOT!" said Danny, squirming. "You're selling powdered jackalope horns! We know all about it!"

Lenny put a large webbed hand over his face.

"Should we gank 'em, boss?" asked Earl. "I don't want to gank anybody, but if we have to, I could use the Chinese Throwing Lanyard of Death—"

"Earl," said Lenny, sounding very tired, "we are *petty* criminals. We do not gank campers. That is not our thing. We'll lock them up, I suppose, and then we can round up the rest of the jackalopes—hopefully they won't have gone far—and after the buyers have left, we'll figure something out."

Danny listened to this and immediately zeroed in on the most important bit.

"There's a Chinese Throwing Lanyard of Death?"

"Yeah!" Earl forgot the headlock long enough to wave his hands in the air in excitement. "It's really cool! You use razor wire—you have to use gloves to weave it—"

"Earl!" said Lenny. "Jackalopes are getting away!"

"Right, boss. Sorry, boss."

Lenny grabbed Danny around the waist with one flabby arm and dragged him away from the door. The remaining jackalopes in the cages put their paws up on the wire bars and gronked frantically.

"No!" Danny kicked out hard, but Lenny was

very large, and years of dodge ball and scavenger hunts apparently make you very strong. He wanted to breathe fire—forget jail, Lenny deserved it!—but he was afraid of hitting one of the jackalopes too. All that fur would probably burn *really well.*

"You know, you could have just left it," said Lenny wearily. "I'm not a vengeful frog. I would have been willing to let bygones be bygones. It's not like I would have had you locked in the cellar or anything. We don't even *have* a cellar. There's a rather large walk-in pantry, but that's as far as it goes."

Danny squirmed under the frog's grip. "You mean you're not going to gank us?"

Lenny sighed. "Do you *know* what happens when a camper gets ganked? The police show up, the FBI shows up, the parents sue, the other parents sue because their precious angel was traumatized, and that's the end of Camp Jackalope. No. I am not going to gank either of you."

Wendell, trying to navigate blindly, ran into a jackalope cage. The occupant kicked out at him.

"No. I am going to send you back to your cabins. The counselors already know better than to listen to you. And when you go screaming to your parents at the end of the week that the head counselor is keeping mythical creatures in the storage shed, I will point out that you are a youngster with a very active imagination, that we were keeping an injured jack*rabbit* in here while it healed, and that you managed to multiply that into a horde of jackalopes. And then I will laugh and pat you on the head—"

JUST *TRY* IT.

"—and agree with your parents that you are quite a handful." The big frog shoved Danny farther into the cabin and folded his arms. Danny rescued Wendell, who was about to wander into a wall. "And then they will apologize for taking so much of my time, and I will suggest that perhaps Camp Jackalope is not the place for you in the future, Dragonbreath."

"Sure I can. I'm an adult. And the adults *always* win." Lenny poked Danny in the chest with a flabby finger. Danny thought he was probably mad enough to breathe fire—he could feel an acidic burn at the back of his throat—but he didn't dare. Lenny was right. There was no way that any grown-up would believe Danny's story, and setting Lenny on fire wouldn't help at *all*.

And then Danny saw something behind Lenny, peeking around the doorway.

It was Spencer. And—oh no, with him, was that—*Jack?*

Danny stifled a groan. If Lenny saw them, he might catch Jack, and when these mysterious buyers showed up, there'd be one more jackalope in the cages, waiting to have his horns ground into powder.

He tried to catch Spencer's eye. "Well, if you've got it all figured out, I guess we should *get going* then . . ."

Lenny was counting jackalopes. "Eight . . . nine . . . hmm?"

"If you've got it all figured out, we should just *get out of here.*" Danny jerked his head at Spencer, hoping he'd get the message.

Spencer grinned like an idiot and waved at him. Danny took a step sideways and saw that Spencer was actually sitting on Jack's back—was he *riding* him? Jack wasn't that much bigger than Spencer, so maybe they were very strong for their size . . .

"Oh no," said Lenny. "You've caused enough trouble for now. I'm gonna march you down to my office and you're going to sit there until after the buyers have come by, and you and Wendell are going to be cleaning lunch trays until the end of camp—"

"Hey, Frogbutt!" yelled Spencer.

Danny covered his eyes. The next time they played video games together, Danny was going to wrap a controller cord around his cousin's stupid *neck.*

Lenny whirled around, saw Spencer, said, "What—?" and then saw Jack.

The head counselor lunged for the jackalope. Jack danced backward, out the door, while Spencer held on to his antlers for dear life. Lenny made a grab for him but missed, probably because Danny had just smacked into the back of his knees, yelling, "Leave him alone!"

(Not even Danny knew whether he was referring to Spencer or Jack, and fortunately, nobody ever asked.)

Lenny lunged forward.

Jack and Spencer ran. The little jackalope was fast, but he was carrying a rider, and they weren't nearly far enough ahead of Lenny for Danny's comfort. He ducked past Earl and gave chase.

A WILD RIDE

Moonlight splashed the campgrounds. Danny could hear the sounds of singing from the direction of the campfire. The dark shape of Lenny ran ahead of him, big webbed feet slapping the ground, and Danny panted as he tried to keep up.

He hoped Lenny couldn't catch Jack.

He hoped Wendell and Christiana could handle Earl.

They passed the other storage shed, the girls' bathroom, and the farthest cabins. Danny could feel a stabbing pain starting in his side. He didn't know how much farther he could run, and if Lenny did something to Spencer . . .

Danny's vision filled up with bright sparkles. That probably wasn't a good sign.

Something next to him said, "Gronk!"

Danny jumped sideways, startled, tripped over a rock, and fell into a bush.

It was another jackalope, and this one was twice the size of Jack.

It gronked again, urgently, then crouched down and gave him a meaningful look.

"You want me to *ride* you? Really?"

"Gronk!"

It didn't need to gronk at him twice.

Danny scrambled onto the jackalope's back. It was a lot smaller than Bandit, and he didn't quite know where to put his feet. He was still trying to figure it out when the jackalope took off at a run.

Riding a jackalope was not like riding a horse. It didn't gallop, it *bounded*. You had no way to steer and only the antlers to hang on to. It was the most exhilarating ride of Danny's life, but he would have given a lot to have stirrups. Every step slammed him hard into the jackalope's backbone—probably not any fun for the jack-alope either, Danny thought—and then he lifted

up again and nearly fell off until the next step slammed him down hard.

He hoped they were gaining on Lenny. He couldn't tell. Holding on was consuming all of his attention.

The trees flashed by. A few times Danny was sure that they were going to collide with a tree trunk, and then the jackalope would wrench to one side and clear the trunk by inches. Undergrowth whipped at his legs.

Danny was very glad when they were out of the forest and into the desert. The rocks slid under the jackalope's paws, but there were fewer things to dodge. The desert was clear and stark in the moonlight.

He caught a glimpse of Lenny ahead of them. The big frog was clearly winded and had slowed to a jog, but Jack and Spencer were barely keeping ahead of him. The little jackalope was not so much bounding as hopping, and Spencer kept shooting terrified glances over his shoulder.

Danny crouched low over his jackalope's back. They were gaining, but would they be fast enough?

"Gotcha now!" cried Lenny.

Jack put on a last, desperate burst of speed, and dodged behind a tall jumble of rocks.

"No!" cried Danny as Lenny closed in.

And then a sea of dark shapes separated themselves from the stones, and moved to encircle Lenny.

Moonlight glittered on a dozen pairs of antlers.

The jackalopes were waiting.

The jackalopes were *not happy.*

"Groo-ooonk!" said Jack.

The other jackalopes didn't say anything. They just moved in closer . . . and closer . . .

Danny's jackalope crouched down and slid Danny off. Danny took a step, realized his legs weren't quite in the same shape they had been when he started, and sat down hard. His jackalope stepped forward to close off Lenny's escape.

WELL.
LOOKS LIKE
THE ADULTS DON'T
ALWAYS WIN,
HUH?

Lenny glared at him over the ring of prongs. "Dragonbreath," he said. "You're *both* trouble. When I get my hands on you—"

A jackalope charged. Lenny jumped as antlers jabbed his backside. The ring of jackalopes moved with him.

"Shoo!" yelled Lenny. "Get out of here! Go awaaaa*aaiiiiieeeeeee!*"

Danny's last sight of counselor Lenny was the frog running across the desert, the ring of jackalopes closing around him, antlers flashing. The frog's yells were quickly swallowed by the night.

Danny exhaled.

"Jack gathered them all up," said Spencer, coming out from behind the rock. He put an arm around Jack's neck. The young jackalope looked exhausted but smug. "Then we just had to lead Lenny back here . . ."

"Spencer, that's awesome!" said Danny.

He stood up. It went a little better this time, although he was still sore in places that he didn't know he had.

WE RODE JACKALOPES! AND WASN'T IT THE AWESOMEST THING EVER? EXCEPT THAT IT KINDA ... HURT ... A LOT ...

YOU'RE TELLIN' ME...

Still, riding the jackalopes really had been cool. And Spencer and Jack really had helped save the day.

Danny looked around, made sure no one was watching—except for the jackalopes, of course—and hugged his cousin. "You did great!"

Spencer grinned and ducked his head. "Yeah. I did, didn't I? I mean, it was just like the one bit in *One Fleece* where the albatross leads the army of—"

Danny sighed and began herding the chattering Spencer back to camp.

AN ALARMING DEVELOPMENT

Meanwhile, back at Camp Jackalope (Your Home on the Range!) Earl and Wendell were staring at each other—or rather, Earl was staring at Wendell, and Wendell was peering nearsightedly at the lizard-shaped blur that was Earl.

"I really don't feel good about this," said Earl apologetically. "But the boss wouldn't want me to let you go."

"Could you help me find my glasses, anyway?" asked Wendell. He knew he had to free the last couple of jackalopes, but at the moment he couldn't tell a jackalope from a giraffe.

"Oh—sure." Earl came around the corner of the table. "I'm really not a bad guy," he told the iguana. "I don't like doing this. But if I don't do what Lenny says, he'll fire me, and it's not as easy to get a lanyard-related job as it used to be."

"Mmm," said Wendell. By touch he managed to find a latch on a cage, and flipped it open. Something inside went "Gronk!" and pushed against the wire.

HEY, CUT THAT OUT!

Wendell hurried blindly down the table and flipped another latch by feel. A jackalope went past him in an antlered blur.

"Kid, I don't want to have to stuff you in the pantry—"

"Oh no, not another one!" Earl rolled his eyes. "And this one's got painted toenails. Look, kid, I don't really want to do this, but I have to. And what are *you* going to do to stop me?"

"This," said Christiana—and pulled the fire alarm.

There was one on every cabin. They had been installed last year after the Bottle Rocket Incident.

When Christiana pulled the alarm, sirens went off all over camp. Lenny had been taking no chances when the system was installed.

It is possible he regretted this later. Certainly Earl did.

Every light in all of Camp Jackalope went on. Campers poured out of the cabins, clutching toothbrushes, towels, and the remains of s'mores, and were greeted by dark horned shapes streaming past them into the night. Any chance of catching the escaping jackalopes was lost as campers milled about aimlessly, looking for the source of the noise. Somebody screamed, and somebody else began to cry.

"Oh crud," said Earl, because Christiana's counselor was running up the pathway, along with the nurse and the woman who served lunch in the camp cafeteria, and all of them were yelling.

ONE OF MY KIDS IS MISSING! SHE DIDN'T COME BACK FROM CAMPFIRE!

"What do we do?"

"I see smoke over by the craft cabin!" said Christiana helpfully, and pointed.

Nobody else saw the smoke, since Christiana had just made it up on the spot, but they all ran that way anyway, and Earl, forgetting that it was all a ruse, yelled, *"The lanyards!"* and ran after them.

Christiana slipped inside the cabin and quickly freed the rest of the jackalopes. "Where did Danny and Spencer go?" she asked.

"It's all a blur," said Wendell gloomily. "Like, literally."

"Hmm."

The last of the jackalopes fled the cabin, stopping to poke Wendell with its nose in a friendly fashion.

"Do you think they're okay?" asked Wendell worriedly as they left the cabin. He was using Christiana as a seeing-eye lizard and trying not to trip on the ground.

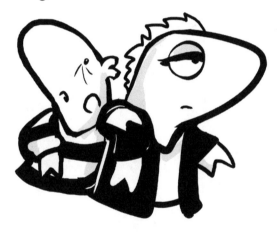

"Actually, they're coming this way. . . ." said Christiana.

Danny and Spencer hurried up.

"Are you okay? You're limping."

"We're fine," said Danny, rubbing his tail. "Just . . . jackalope backbones . . . Look, I'll explain later. You wouldn't *believe* the story I've got to tell you . . ."

TRIUMPH ON THE RANGE

Lenny was gone the next day. When somebody asked where he was, the counselors said that he'd had a family emergency and been called away suddenly. Earl was still around, but he was extremely jumpy and yelped whenever anybody opened the door to the craft cabin. Wendell's glasses eventually turned up in the lost and found, and that was more or less that.

"It wasn't a family emergency," said Christiana smugly, a day later.

"Well, *duh*," said Danny.

"No, I mean I overheard the lunch lady talking to the nurse." (This was technically true, although Christiana had been hiding behind the Dumpster with the express purpose of overhearing this particular conversation.) "Lenny's been *arrested*."

"No way!"

"They said there were 'financial irregularities' in the bookkeeping. Two police officers came in a car and took him away!" said Christiana happily. "Apparently Lenny had been stealing money from the camp, and there was a big audit coming, so he was desperate for money!"

"I bet he was selling jackalope horns to make money to cover his tracks," said Wendell.

"That jerk!" Danny couldn't believe it. "He stole money AND jackalopes? Man, I hope he goes to jail *forever*."

"No, no, no!" Christiana waved her hands. "That's not the best part! You're not going to believe this! Guess where they found him?"

"Way!" Christiana grinned. "The nurse'll tell Heidi, and it'll be all over the camp in an hour. When I left, they were already making up a camp song about it."

A door slammed. Danny looked up, surprised, and saw that Earl was gone from the craft cabin. A minute later, the sound of a car engine started over in the parking lot, followed by a screech of tires.

"What was *his* problem?" asked Spencer.

"Bet he's worried about being named as an accomplice," said Christiana.

"He'll never make a lanyard in this town again," said Wendell.

After that, there was only one thing left to do.

Well, there were actually a lot of things to do—excuses to make and sleeping bags to roll up (they never seemed to roll up as tightly as when they went in) and the big final trail-ride. Danny enjoyed this even more than usual. Bandit might not be as fast as a jackalope, but he was a heckuva lot more comfortable.

Danny was so happy, he felt like singing . . . just not the Camp Jackalope theme song.

HOME,
HOME ON THE RAAANGE,
WHERE THE DRAGONS
AND JACKALOPES PLAAAAY...
WHERE WENDELL'S A NERD,
AND SPENCER'S BEEN HEARD,
AND CHRISTIANA COMPLAINS
LOUDLY ALL DAAAAY...!

But on the last night of camp, during the big final campfire, when everybody sang the camp song (all twenty-seven verses, plus two new ones about criminals on the girls' bathroom, which didn't rhyme very well but were greeted with shouts of laughter anyway) the four heroic jack-alope rescuers slipped away into the desert.

They went down the canyon to the little hole in the rock and waited.

One by one, the stars came out—and then, just when they'd started to think that no one was coming—

"Look!" said Danny, pointing.

"They made it . . ." whispered Spencer.

"They did," said Christiana.

The heads began to vanish, one at a time, as the jackalopes turned and loped into the desert. Danny caught the gleam of a familiar whistle hanging around one jackalope's neck like a trophy.

In a little knot under the saguaro, four jack-alopes waited. Two of them were eyeing Danny and his friends warily. The third was listening to Jack gronk and had a strangely familiar expression.

GRONK–GRONK GRONK, GRONK GRONKY GRONK . . .

"No wonder Spencer could understand him," whispered Wendell. "What do you want to bet that Jack's the rabbit equivalent of your cousin?"

"Do jackalopes even *get* cable?" asked Danny.

Jack finally finished talking the other jackalope's ear off, then came up to each kid in turn and rubbed his nose against their hands.

"His family," said Spencer. "We *did* get them back! Oh, Jack, I'm so happy!" He hugged his friend, and the horned rabbit hugged him back.

But later, after the jackalopes had melted into the night and they began the long walk back to camp, Spencer didn't look happy. In fact, he looked like he was crying.

"Hey, Spence," said Danny, putting an arm around him. "It's okay."

"I'll *miss* him," Spencer said. "I know he's a wild animal, and I know I couldn't keep him, but he was my *friend*. And now I'll never see him again!"

"Of course you will," said Danny. "You'll see him next summer. I promise. *And* the summer after that."

"Definitely," said Wendell. "You're coming back, right? I mean, we *always* come back to Camp Jackalope."

"Maybe next year we'll get to be in the same cabin," said Danny.

"You mean it?" said Spencer. "The same cabin?"

"If you *promise* not to tell me about any more TV shows . . ." said Danny, and the two dragons and their friends walked up the slope and back to the campfire.

Calling all artists!

DRAGONBREATH

Create-Your-Own-Comic
CONTEST!

Visit Penguin.com/Dragonbreath
for the full Official Rules and to
download and print an entry form!

Enter for the opportunity to have your Dragonbreath comic published in a future Dragonbreath book! Plus, the winner will receive copies of all the Dragonbreath series books, signed by the author, Ursula Vernon (Approximate Retail Value: $91.00). No purchase necessary. Open to residents of the fifty United States and the District of Columbia, ages 7–13. Contest begins March 20, 2012. Entries must be postmarked on or before June 25, 2012 and received on or by July 2, 2012. Judging will take place on or about July 9, 2012, and will be based on content, creativity, and how well the Dragonbreath characters are represented. Void where prohibited by law.